On With the Show!

Written by Gare Thompson

STECK-VAUGHN
COMPANY
ELEMENTARY • SECONDARY • ADULT • LIBRARY

Contents

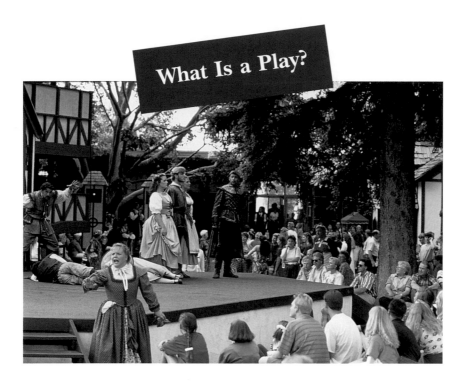

What Is a Play?

A play is a story acted out on stage. When the curtains go up, the actors tell the story with words, songs, or dances. A play can be funny or sad. A play can be real or make-believe.

The best part about a play is that you can see the story as it is told. You watch the **actors** become the people in the story. This is how a story comes to life.

Kinds of Plays

There are different kinds of plays. Some plays are funny. The actors say or do things that make people laugh. A funny play is called a **comedy**. Some plays are about things that happen to people. A play may tell about many people or just about one person.

Another kind of play is a **puppet** play. It has puppets as the actors. People stand behind the stage and make the puppets move and talk. It is fun to put on a puppet play.

The puppets turn into actors on the puppet stage.

A long time ago, all plays were done outside. People sat on a hillside to watch the play. The actors were down below on the stage, but often they were hard to see. The actors were far away from the people who watched them.

In these shows, the actors often wore large masks. The masks showed a big smile or a big frown. That way, people who sat far away could see if each actor was playing a happy part or a sad part.

The crowd watches a play on a hillside.

Some plays have singing and dancing. These plays are **musicals**. The actors in musicals know how to sing. Sometimes they sing alone, but sometimes many people sing together.

In a musical, the actors also know how to dance. Some musicals have tap dancing, jazz dancing, ballet, or even square dancing. Musicals are fun to watch as the actors dance on stage.

Actors sing and dance in this musical.

Who Works on a Play?

Many people work on a play. Each person works as part of a team to make the play fun for the people who watch. Most plays start with a good writer. But some plays are written by many writers who work together.

The writers choose the words that the actors will say. The words are the **dialogue** of the play. The writers also tell where the actors should be and what they should do. The actors need to know when to come on stage and when to leave.

These actors are practicing their dialogue on stage.

The actors who are in a play are a very important group of people. The actors seem to become the **characters** in the story. They pretend to be someone else when they are on the stage. Often very nice people play the parts of mean characters. If they are good actors, you will believe they really are mean.

Actors have to learn all their own lines. They also learn what the other actors say. This helps them know when to say their own lines.

This actor plays the part of a mean character.

Who is the boss when people are working on a play? It is the **director**. A director is the person who tells everyone else how to do the play. Directors help the actors say their lines at just the right time. They tell the actors where to stand on the stage.

Directors help plan the **scenery** that will be placed on the stage. They also choose which **props** to use. They plan what each scene will look like and how to make it happen. The director decides who will do what to make the best play.

The director decides what will happen in a play.

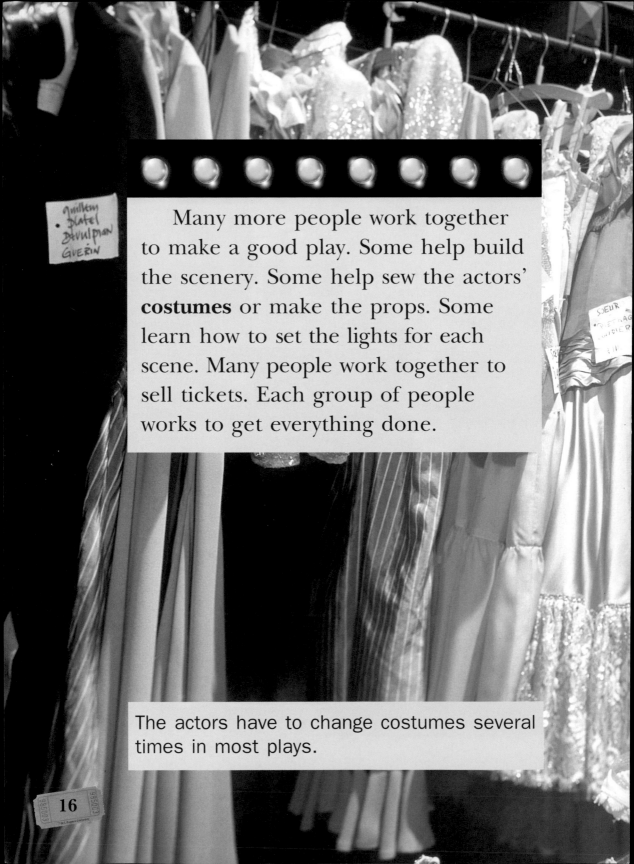

Many more people work together to make a good play. Some help build the scenery. Some help sew the actors' **costumes** or make the props. Some learn how to set the lights for each scene. Many people work together to sell tickets. Each group of people works to get everything done.

The actors have to change costumes several times in most plays.

In a play with music, there is always a band, or **orchestra.** The people in the orchestra play the music. They help the actors sing along. They help the dancers move on the right beat. They even help the people who are watching feel happy during the happy parts.

Some of the people in the orchestra may play the trumpet, flute, or violin. Others may play the piano or tuba. They all work together to make the music great.

The orchestra and actors take a bow.

There are other sounds in plays besides music. Think about the sounds around you. What are some sounds that make a school sound like a school? What are some sounds that make you think you are outside on a summer day?

In a play, these kinds of sounds are the **sound effects**. If the actors say that the phone is ringing now, they need a sound effect for a phone ringing. The sound effects make a play seem real.

A sound effect makes this phone call seem real.

How to Write a Play

Where can you get ideas for a play? A play might be about something that happened to you. Or it could be from a favorite story you have read. Sometimes a play even comes from a news article about something that has happened. Just remember that plays are another way of telling a story. You can use any ideas you have for a story to write a play.

These writers are working together to write a play.

A good play is like a good story. A play should have a beginning, a middle, and an end. Each part of the play can happen in a different place. Or it might all happen in one place. You'll need scenery and props for each scene.

If you want to write a play about your day, the first part might happen in your home. The middle part might happen in your classroom. The last part might take place on the playground after school. Remember that you can use dialogue, dances, and songs in your play.

These children are painting scenery for a play.

Think about the characters who will be in your play. Will you need a mother or a father character? Will you need a teacher or some other adults? How many people of your age will be in your play?

Make a list of everyone who will be on the stage. Then write a short note about each of the characters. Tell their age and how they fit in the play. You might write:

Tom, age 8, Adam's best friend.

Once you know the characters, think about the dialogue. What do you want the characters to say to each other?

This musical has three characters.

Next, write your play and read it to yourself. Be sure that it makes sense from start to finish. Check that your list of characters includes everyone in the play. Make sure that you don't have too many scenes. Rewrite the parts that need to be more clear.

Then let some friends read your play. Ask if it makes sense to them. Ask if they can picture the actions as they read it.

Ask some friends to read your play.

What will you do next? It is time to put on your play. Ask some people to be your actors. Plan what they will wear. Think about the props you will need. Ask your friends to help you with the props, costumes, and scenery.

Then it's show time. Put on your play for your family or for friends. When the people watching the play start to clap, you'll feel so proud! On with the show!

These actors are putting on their play in the backyard.

Glossary

actors   people who act out parts in a play

characters   people who a play is about

comedy   a funny play

costumes   what the actors wear

dialogue   words the actors say

director   the boss of a play

musicals   plays with singing and dancing

orchestra   people who play the music

props   things the actors use on stage

puppet   a doll with parts that move

scenery   painted pictures of places where actions take place in a play

sound effects   sounds that make a play seem real